The Toolbox

by

Anne & Harlow Rockwell

Macmillan Publishing Company
New York

Macmillan Publishing Company, 866 Third Avenue, New York, NY 10022
Collier Macmillan Canada Inc.

Library of Congress catalog card number: 72-119836

10   9   8

The pictures in this book are full-color watercolor paintings.
The text was hand lettered by the artist.

For Oliver

In my cellar there is a toolbox.
It is dark brown where hands
have touched it.

It has a saw

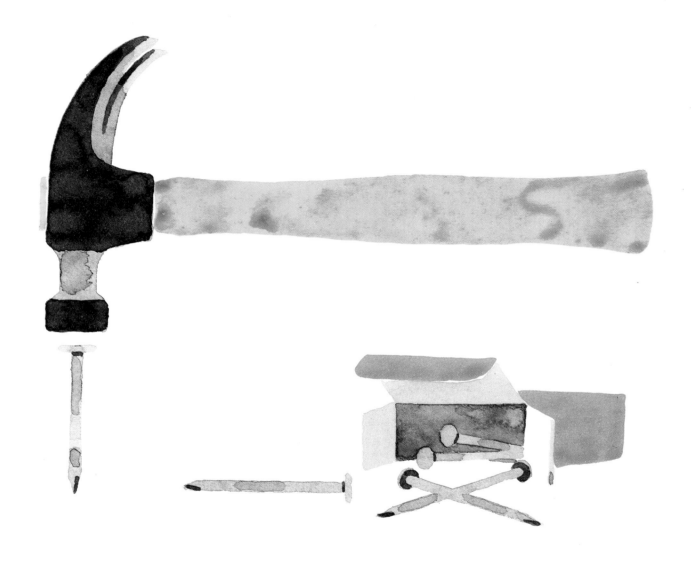

and a hammer and nails,

and a drill
that goes around and around

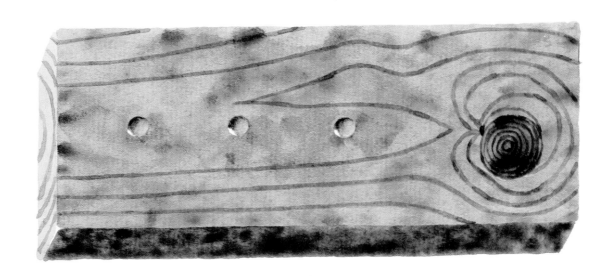

and makes holes in wood.

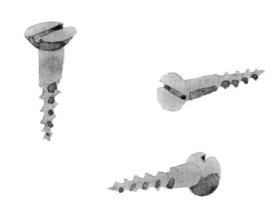

It has screws and a screwdriver,

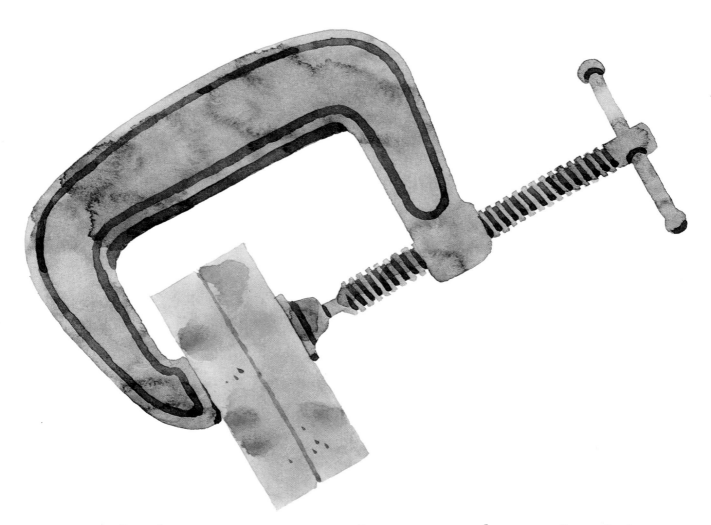

and there is a clamp that holds
pieces of wood together.

There is a big, strong wrench

that turns the big, fat nuts
and bolts,

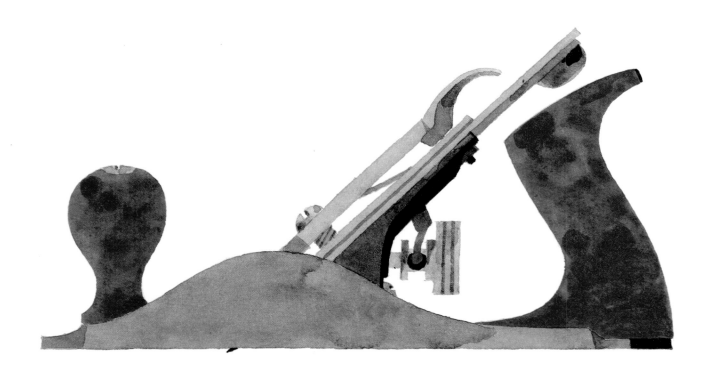

and there is a plane that
smooths wood

and makes curly shavings.

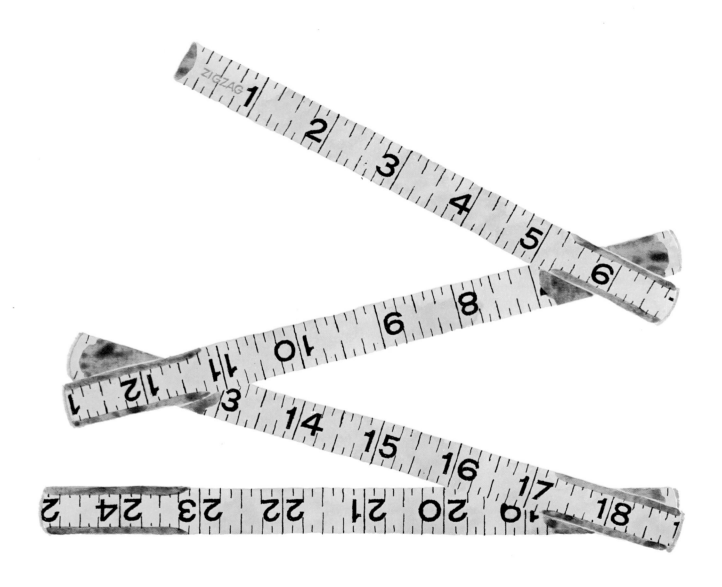

There is a ruler that measures.

There are pliers that pinch.

There is sandpaper to smooth
wood and plaster.

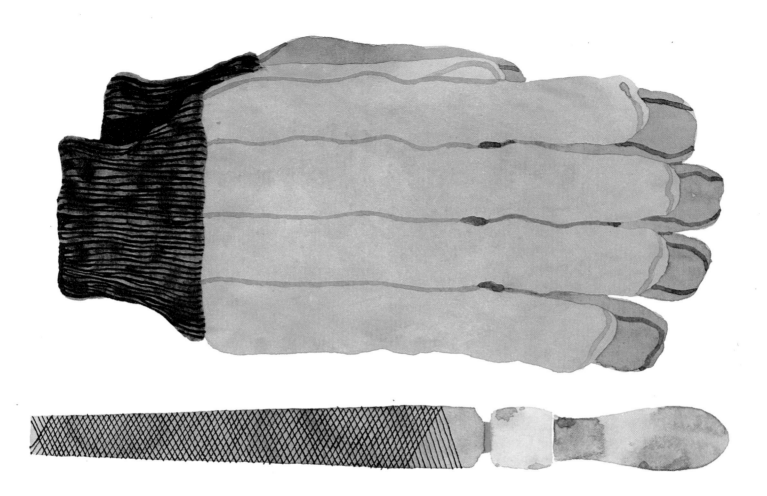

There are work gloves, and there is a file to rub on rough edges of metal to make them smooth.

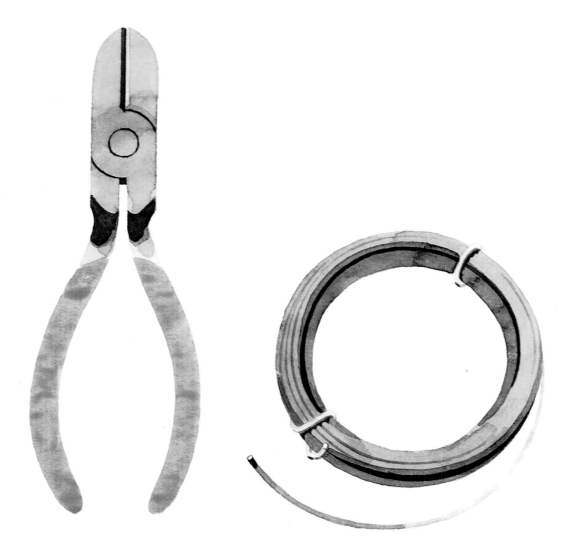

There are sharp wire cutters
and a roll of wire.

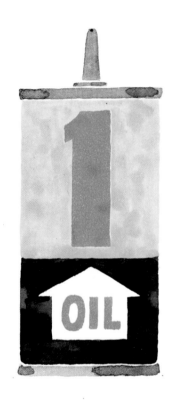

There is an oil can with
a tiny hole.

It is my father's toolbox.